HARES AND RABBITS

BY RYAN GALE

The Child's World®
childsworld.com

Published by The Child's World®
1980 Lookout Drive • Mankato, MN 56003-1705
800-599-READ • www.childsworld.com

Photographs ©: Mriya Wildlife/Shutterstock Images, cover (hare), 2, 8, 20, 24 (hare); Shutterstock Images, cover (rabbit), 3, 5, 10, 16, 21, 24 (rabbit); Volodymyr Burdiak/Shutterstock Images, 6; Howard Sandler/Shutterstock Images, 9; Pattaya Photography/Shutterstock Images, 13; William Booth/Shutterstock Images, 14; Kassia Marie Ott/Shutterstock Images, 17; Deep Desert Photography/Shutterstock Images, 19

ISBN 9781503835917
LCCN 2019943000

Printed in the United States of America

ABOUT THE AUTHOR

Ryan Gale is an author and artist living in Minnesota. He enjoys reading and writing about nature.

TABLE OF CONTENTS

CHAPTER

1

Furry Hoppers

A furry animal hops into a bush. It has long ears. It has a short tail. Is it a hare or a rabbit? How are they different?

Both rabbits and hares eat only plants.

Hares use their long legs and long ears to help keep them safe.

CHAPTER

2

Hares

Hares have long back legs and small tails. Their long legs help them run fast. They also have long ears. Big ears help them hear **predators**. Hares can run away if they hear one.

Hares have short fur. Some hares change color in winter. Their fur changes from brown to white. This makes it hard for predators to see hares in the snow.

Hares live in **nests** above ground. Most live in open areas with few trees. This lets them see predators that are far away. Hares usually live alone. They can be very shy. They are wild animals.

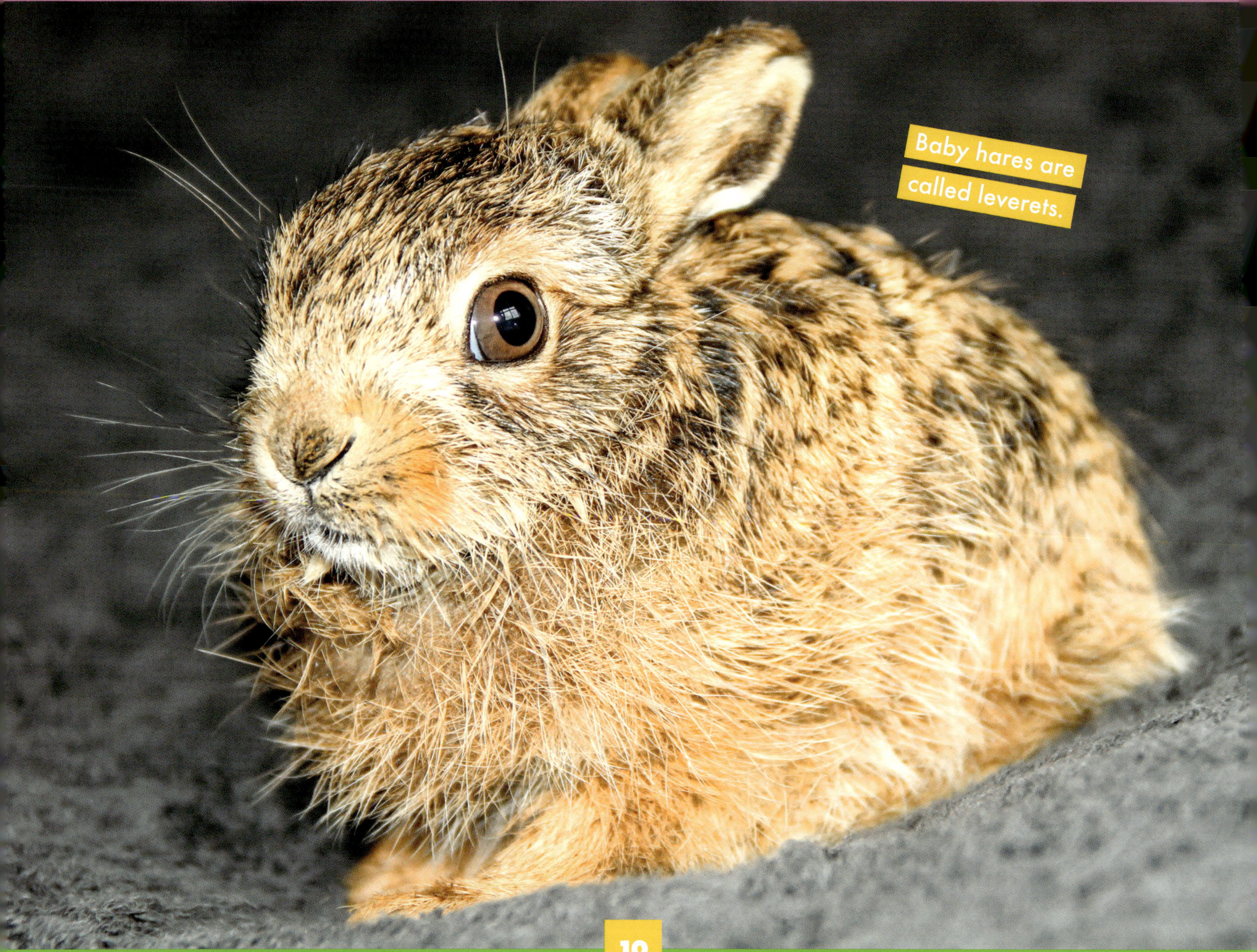
Baby hares are
called leverets.

Hares are born with fur. The fur keeps them warm. They are born with their eyes open. They can hop soon after birth. Baby hares need little help from their parents.

CHAPTER 3

Rabbits

Rabbits have small tails and short, strong back legs. Their strong legs help them hop quickly. Their legs also help them dig. Rabbits have long ears. Some have long fur. Most have short fur. Their fur stays the same color all year.

Rabbits use their legs
for digging.

Rabbits tend to live in groups.

Most rabbits live in underground **burrows**. They like areas with trees and bushes. They use them to hide from predators. Rabbits are **social** animals. They live in small groups. Rabbits can make good pets.

Rabbits are helpless when they are born. They are born without fur. Their parents help them stay warm. They cannot see or hop for several days after birth.

Baby rabbits are called kits.

CHAPTER

4

What's the Difference?

Hares have long back legs. Rabbits have short and strong back legs. Hares try to outrun predators. Rabbits prefer to hide. Rabbits live in burrows. Hares live in nests above ground. Baby rabbits are helpless when they are born. Baby hares are not.

Hares and rabbits are very similar. Their names are often mixed up. The jackrabbit is a hare. The Belgian hare is a rabbit. Both hares and rabbits are exciting animals.

HARES

- Live in nests above ground
- Run from predators
- Live alone

RABBITS

Long ears
• Live in burrows underground
• Hide from predators
• Live in small groups
Fur color remains the same
Short back legs

GLOSSARY

burrows (BUR-rowz) Burrows are holes or tunnels made by animals for shelter. Rabbits live in burrows.

nests (NESTS) Nests are aboveground homes that animals create. Hares flatten grass to make comfortable nests.

predators (PRED-i-turz) Predators are animals that hunt and eat other animals. Rabbits like to hide from predators.

social (SO-shul) To be social is to spend time with others. Rabbits are social and live in groups, but hares tend to live alone.

TO LEARN MORE

IN THE LIBRARY

Chung, Liz. *Inside Rabbit Burrows*. New York, NY: PowerKids Press, 2016.

Mattern, Joanne. *Hares and Rabbits*. Egremont, MA: Red Chair Press, 2017.

Phillips, Dee. *Snowshoe Hare*. New York, NY: Bearport Publishing, 2015.

ON THE WEB

Visit our website for links about hares and rabbits:
childsworld.com/links

Note to Parents, Teachers, and Librarians: We routinely verify our Web links to make sure they are safe and active sites. So encourage your readers to check them out!

ACTIVITY

Draw a picture of a hare and a rabbit. Your picture should clearly show the differences between the hare and the rabbit. Look at pages 20 and 21 for help.

INDEX